Kitty Princess

AND THE

Newspaper Dress

**BY TREVOR DICKINSON
AND EMMA CARLOW**

ORCHARD BOOKS

For Ella and Lucy.

A special thanks to Jo for all her help and encouragement,
and also for being such a brilliant Fairy Godmouse.

T.D.

For my dear grandmas.

E.C.

ORCHARD BOOKS
96 Leonard Street, London EC2A 4XD
Orchard Books Australia
32/45-51 Huntley Street, Alexandria, NSW 2015
ISBN 1 84362 138 X (hardback)
ISBN 1 84362 358 7 (paperback)
First published in Great Britain in 2003
First paperback publication in 2004
Text and illustrations © Emma Carlow and Trevor Dickinson 2003
The right of Emma Carlow and Trevor Dickinson to be identified as
the authors and illustrators of this work has been asserted by them
in accordance with the Copyright, Designs and Patents Act, 1988.
A CIP catalogue record for this book is available from the British Library.
1 2 3 4 5 6 7 8 9 10 (hardback)
1 2 3 4 5 6 7 8 9 10 (paperback)
Printed in Belgium

Meet Kitty Princess.
She likes to think that she's the prettiest cat in town.
But once upon a time she was the rudest!

When Kitty Princess wanted something, did she say 'please'?
No, she shouted, **"THAT'S AN ORDER!"**
And when she got what she wanted,
she didn't even say 'thank you'.
How rude!

My name's Fairy Godmouse.
I look after Kitty Princess.
I'm patient, caring and kind –
if I don't mind saying so myself.

But sometimes Kitty was so rude
even I thought enough was enough.
Like the morning I was woken by Kitty shouting...

"GET ME THE BEST DRESS IN THE WORLD FOR PRINCE QUINCE'S BALL TONIGHT, AND THAT'S AN **ORDER!**"

Well, I tried my best, but my
mousey magic isn't brilliant
before breakfast.

"Your spells are rubbish!" yowled Kitty.
"I could do better myself."

"Kitty Princess, you are so rude!"
I told her. "Say you're sorry."

"No," said Kitty. "Won't."

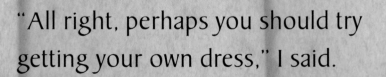

"All right, perhaps you should try
getting your own dress," I said.

"FINE!" shouted Kitty.
"That's easy, just watch me!"

Kitty stomped into town. I followed at
a safe distance, so she wouldn't see me.

You see, Kitty had never been shopping before and
I thought it could be fun to watch.
Kitty went into the first shop she saw…

VEGETABLES

to buy some shoes.

"Make me a pair of your prettiest
shoes by teatime," demanded Kitty.
"But madam, we only sell fruit
and vegetables!" cried the greengrocer.

Kitty wouldn't listen.
"THAT'S AN ORDER!
Shoes by teatime, **OR ELSE!"**
she snapped as she swept out of the shop.

Next, Kitty went into a café.
"Make me your most precious jewellery by teatime," she shouted.
"I'm sorry, did you say jewellery?" asked the waitress.
"WHAT ELSE WOULD I BE ASKING FOR?" shouted Kitty.
"But Miss–" the waitress tried to reply.

"THAT'S AN ORDER!" yelled Kitty.

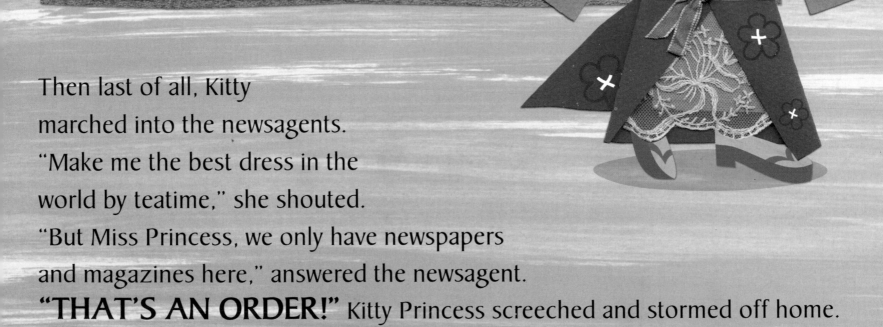

Then last of all, Kitty
marched into the newsagents.
"Make me the best dress in the
world by teatime," she shouted.
"But Miss Princess, we only have newspapers
and magazines here," answered the newsagent.
"THAT'S AN ORDER!" Kitty Princess screeched and stormed off home.

At teatime, Kitty skipped back into town.
She was looking forward to being the
prettiest princess at the party...
she was in for a BIG surprise.

She went into the greengrocers.
"Here are your shoes, madam," said the greengrocer. "Just as you ordered."
"What?" cried Kitty, taking the shoes.
There was no time to argue – the ball was about to start.

She hurried to the café.
"Where's my jewellery?" she yelled.
"Right here," said the waitress.
"Eurgh! It's horrible," cried Kitty,
as she ran from the shop,
grabbing the jewellery.

Takeaway

1 tiara
1 necklace
2 earrings

Must be ready
by teatime!

one dress
for Kitty Princess

Now Kitty was worried
about her dress. She ran
to the newsagent.
Kitty couldn't believe her eyes.
Whatever the newsagent had
made, it certainly wasn't the
best dress in the world.

When Kitty Princess got home,
she tried on her party outfit.
She didn't look pretty.
She just looked plain silly, but
there was no time to change.
Kitty would have to go to the
ball wearing the worst
dress in the world.

One dress for Kitty Princess

When she arrived at Prince Quince's palace,
the butler would not let her in.
"I have never seen anyone dressed so
ridiculously in my entire life," he said.
"I simply cannot allow you to enter."

But everyone else was going to the ball – the greengrocer,
the waitress and even the newsagent.
Everyone but Kitty.

Kitty Princess didn't know what to do.
Everything had gone wrong. Kitty looked very sad indeed.
"I wish I hadn't been so rude to everyone. It's all my fault,"
she wailed.

"FAIRY GODMOUSE, PLEASE COME BACK.
I'M SORRY!"

Did you hear that? Kitty Princess actually said 'sorry'!
I decided it was time I appeared.
"Oh, Fairy Godmouse, I'll never call your spells rubbish again.
From now on I'll try to be a much nicer princess."

I gave her a big
hug and said,
"Is there anyone
else you should be
saying sorry to?"

"Well," sniffed Kitty, "I'm sorry for being rude to you, Greengrocer." And as she said sorry, her vegetable shoes turned into the prettiest and most dazzling slippers ever worn.

Everyone gasped.

"I'm sorry to you too, Waitress," she called. And Kitty Princess' nasty jewellery turned into the most exquisite and precious jewellery ever seen.

Everyone oooed.

"And I'm very sorry to you as well, Newsagent," cried Kitty. And no sooner had the words left her lips than her newspaper dress changed into the **BEST DRESS IN THE WHOLE WORLD!**

Everyone ahhhed.

"Thank you, Fairy Godmouse!" whispered Kitty,
as the butler let her into the ball.

Kitty looked beautiful –
if I don't mind saying so
myself. So beautiful, in fact,
that Prince Quince marched
straight up to her and said...

"YOU THERE! I ORDER YOU TO DANCE WITH ME NOW!"

HOW RUDE!
Well, I couldn't
allow that, could I?

So I turned him into a frog.